TITLE: I Want My Mummy!

AUTHOR: Nancy Krulik

IMPRINT: Aladdin

ON-SALE DATE: 04/13/2021

ISBN: 978-1-5344-5396-8 (pbk); 978-1-5344-5397-5 (hc)

FORMAT: Simultaneous paperback and hardcover

PRICE: $5.99 US/$7.99 CAN (pbk); $17.99 US/$23.99 CAN (hc)

AGES: 7–10

PAGES: 144

Please send a URL for any online coverage related to this book to:
childrenspublicity@simonandschuster.com.
Please send two copies of any review or mention of this book to:
Simon & Schuster Children's Publicity Department
1230 Avenue of the Americas, 4th Floor
New York, NY 10020
212/698-2808

Aladdin • Atheneum Books for Young Readers
Beach Lane Books • Beyond Words • Denene Millner Books
Libros para niños • Little Simon • Margaret K. McElderry Books
Paula Wiseman Books • Salaam Reads
Simon & Schuster Books for Young Readers
Simon Pulse • Simon Spotlight

★ Also in the ★
MS. FROGBOTTOM'S FIELD TRIPS series

Book 2: *Long Time, No Sea Monster*

MS. FROGBOTTOM'S FIELD TRIPS

✦ I WANT MY MUMMY! ✦

By **TONY**, *As told to* **NANCY KRULIK**
Illustrated by **HARRY BRIGGS**

ALADDIN

New York London Toronto Sydney New Delhi

ALADDIN
An imprint of Simon & Schuster Children's Publishing Division
1230 Avenue of the Americas, New York, New York 10020
First Aladdin paperback edition April 2021
Text copyright © 2021 by Nancy Krulik
Illustrations copyright © 2021 by Harry Briggs
Also available in an Aladdin hardcover edition.
All rights reserved, including the right of reproduction in whole or in part in any form.
ALADDIN and related logo are registered trademarks of Simon & Schuster, Inc.
For information about special discounts for bulk purchases, please contact
Simon & Schuster Special Sales at 1-866-506-1949 or business@simonandschuster.com.
The Simon & Schuster Speakers Bureau can bring authors to your live event.
For more information or to book an event contact the Simon & Schuster Speakers
Bureau at 1-866-248-3049 or visit our website at www.simonspeakers.com.
Cover designed by Karin Paprocki
Interior designed by Mike Rosamilia
The illustrations for this book were rendered in TK.
The text of this book was set in Neutraface Slab Text.
Manufactured in the United States of America 0321 OFF
2 4 6 8 10 9 7 5 3 1
Library of Congress Control Number 2020936642
ISBN 978-1-5344-5397-5 (hc)
ISBN 978-1-5344-5396-8 (pbk)
ISBN 978-1-5344-5398-2 (eBook)

For my mummy *and* my daddy,
Gladys and Steve Krulik
—N. K.

WELCOME TO CLASS 4A.

We have a warning for you:

BEWARE OF THE MAP.

Our classroom probably looks a lot like yours. We have chairs, desks, a whiteboard, and artwork on the walls. And of course we have our teacher, Ms. Frogbottom.

Actually, our teacher is the reason why things sometimes get strange around here. Because Ms. Frogbottom is kind of *different*.

For starters, she carries around a backpack. It looks like any other pack, but somehow strange things always seem to be popping out of it. You don't have to worry about most of the stuff our teacher carries. But if she reaches into her pack and pulls out her giant map, beware. That map is *magic*. It has the power to lift us right out of our classroom and drop us in some faraway place. Somehow, no matter where we go, we wind up meeting frightening creatures none of us ever believed were real—and getting into all sorts of trouble.

You don't have to be *too* scared,

though. Things always seem to turn out okay for us in the end. Or at least they have *so far*. . . .

Your new pals,

Aiden, Emma, Oliver, Olivia, Sofia, and Tony

MS. FROGBOTTOM'S FiELD TRiP DO'S AND DON'TS

- Do stay together.

- Don't take photos. You can't experience the big world through a tiny camera hole.

- Don't bring home souvenirs. We want to leave the places we visit exactly as we found them.

- Don't use the word "weird." The people, places, and food we experience are just different from what you are used to.

- Do have fun!

1

YOU KNOW THAT SKIN THAT STICKS OUT from the sides of your fingernails? The kind that looks like pieces of shredded strings?

I hate that skin. Which is why I'm always picking at it.

It makes my mother crazy when I pick. But stringy skin is really annoying. So I keep picking.

And picking.

And picking.

Luckily, my mom's not here to yell at me. I'm in school, waiting for the bell to ring and for my teacher, Ms. Frogbottom, to show up.

Ms. Frogbottom doesn't scold me for picking at the skin around my fingernails. Or at least she hasn't yet.

"Hey, Tony!" my best friend, Oliver,

says as he and his twin sister, Olivia, walk into the classroom.

Oliver hangs his jacket and his backpack on a hook and walks over to my desk. "How was your weekend? Did your cousin take you to see that movie about summer camp?"

"Yeah," I reply. "It was okay."

"Just okay?" Olivia asks, butting into our conversation. "We loved it."

"I liked most of it," I explain. "Just not the part where the bear shows up while they're making s'mores. That scared me."

Did I mention that I hate being scared?

"Oliver and I had our fencing competition on Saturday," Olivia says. "Guess who came in first place?"

Olivia is wearing a huge gold-colored

plastic medal around her neck. Which, of course, means *she* came in first.

I have a feeling Olivia is just wearing the medal to annoy Oliver. I don't know how he puts up with her.

"Check out Sofia," Oliver says, changing the subject. "She's already got her math book open."

I don't know why Oliver sounds surprised. Sofia is the class brain. She's always got her nose in a book. Or in her tablet, looking something up.

Okay, you can't really have your nose in a tablet. But you know what I mean.

Sofia is so busy solving a math problem—just for *fun*—that she doesn't even look up at the sound of her name.

"Do you know why the math book was always upset?" Olivia asks Oliver.

"Because it had so many problems!" Oliver answers her. The twins start laughing hysterically.

"Ms. Frogbottom's coming!" Suddenly my classmate Aiden, who has been standing near the door, shouts out a warning. He races over to his desk and sits in his seat.

The twins sit down too. Now we're all in our places, with bright shiny faces, except...

"Emma!" Aiden exclaims. "Sit down. You know how mad Ms. Frogbottom gets if we're not all seated when she gets here."

I look over at the window. Emma is staring at her reflection in the glass. She's moving her head around and making funny expressions. Smiles. Frowns. And something that looks like duck lips.

"Emma, hurry." Aiden sounds worried. I don't blame him. I don't want Ms. Frogbottom to be in a bad mood right at the start of the day.

Emma stops staring at herself long enough to glare at Aiden. "Are you talking to me? Because if you are, my name's not 'Emma.' It's 'Rainbow.'"

I'm not surprised by that. Last Friday, Emma told everyone she'd changed her name to "Starshine." And a few days before that, it was "Moonglow."

I'm just sticking with "Emma."

"'Rainbow' is a much better name for a painter," she explains.

"I thought you were going to be an actress when you grew up," Olivia says.

"I can be both," Emma replies.

"Fine," Aiden huffs. "You gotta sit down, *Rainbow*."

Emma—or *Rainbow*—takes her seat just as Ms. Frogbottom walks into the room.

"Good morning, Class 4A," our teacher greets us as she puts her backpack down on the floor beside her desk.

"Good morning, Ms. Frogbottom," we answer.

Ms. Frogbottom isn't the kind of teacher to waste time asking us how our weekends were. She's the kind of teacher who gets right to work. Which is why she is already writing the

WOTD—that stands for "Word of the Day"—on the board.

"Ms. Frogbottom, the bell hasn't rung yet," Olivia reminds our teacher.

Bad move.

Ms. Frogbottom shoots her a look. Olivia sinks down in her seat and starts copying the Word of the Day into her notebook.

Arachnophobia (noun): Fear of spiders.

That will be an easy one for me to remember. I'm scared of spiders.

"Speaking of spiders," Ms. Frogbottom says, "I hope you all did your homework and read chapter three in *Charlotte's Web*, because . . ."

Gulp. We had reading homework over the weekend?

Maybe Ms. Frogbottom assigned it while I was watching that freaky cockroach walk along the windowsill? Because I wasn't really listening to her then.

". . . pop quiz."

I'm listening now. "Pop quiz" are two words I really dread. Especially because I didn't read chapter three.

I start picking nervously at the skin around my fingernails again. Why did I have to get the new fourth-grade teacher this year? Ms. Frogbottom isn't like any of the other teachers here at Left Turn Alleyway Elementary. I bet those teachers don't give weekend homework or surprise quizzes. And don't even get me started on how Ms. Frogbottom is always talking about the "magic of field trips."

Now I'm *biting* at the skin around my fingernails. I pull hard at one really annoying skin-string with my teeth.

Ow!

Uh-oh. I'm bleeding.

"Hey!" I exclaim. "Anybody got a Band-Aid?"

Ms. Frogbottom stops talking and stares at me.

Oops. I just called out without raising my hand.

I brace myself for a warning. Or worse.

Surprisingly, Ms. Frogbottom smiles. "I don't have one, Tony," she tells me. "Although, I do know a place where you can find lots of bandages."

Ms. Frogbottom reaches into her backpack and pulls out a giant *map*. A map so huge that there's no way it could possibly fit into that pack. But it does.

I wish I'd never asked for that Band-Aid. I should have just let myself bleed all over the place. Because I know that map. It's not a regular map. It's a *magic* map. A map that can take us any place in the world.

I'm just glad Ms. Frogbottom doesn't pull out that map every day. If she did, I'd never come to school. Because every time she points to a place on that thing, something scary happens.

Like that time Sofia almost got captured by a muldjewangk monster in Australia. If the monster had gotten her, it would have been awful. Muldjewangk monsters cover their victims with ooey-gooey, pus-filled blisters that pop up all over!

Then there was the day in Greenland when Emma twisted her ankle running from a tupilaq statue that had come to life and was trying to make her his prisoner.

I sure hope we don't go somewhere cold this time. I only have a T-shirt on.

Ms. Frogbottom is pointing to some-place on the Magic Map. I can't tell where. My hands are over my eyes.

Even through my fingers I can see a giant flash of light glowing in the class-room. My body feels weightless, and I think my feet have just left the ground.

It's like I'm flying in space. And then . . .

"WHOA!" OLIVER EXCLAIMS.

"Double whoa!" Olivia adds.

I feel sunlight beating down on the back of my neck. Wherever the Magic Map has taken us is hot. *Very* hot. It must be a hundred degrees out here.

I move my hands from my eyes and look around. There's nothing but sand. It's like we're at the beach—except there's no water anywhere.

"I don't see any Band-Aids," Emma says.

I was just thinking the same thing.

Ms. Frogbottom looks at me. "Do you still need a bandage, Tony?"

I look down at my finger. It's not bleeding anymore. "I'm okay," I tell her.

That's not exactly true. My finger's okay. But I'm not. It's so hot out. A big glob of sticky, salty sweat just leaked down from my nose and into my mouth. Yuck.

Ms. Frogbottom reaches into her backpack and pulls out a pile of hats and some sunscreen. "You need to protect yourselves from the sun here," she tells us.

"Where's *here*?" Aiden asks.

Sofia starts typing something into her tablet.

Yep. That's right. Sofia brought her tablet. Which doesn't surprise me, since I've never seen Sofia *without* her tablet. I bet she sleeps with it.

"Judging by all the sand, heat, and lack of clouds, I'd say we're in a desert," Sofia tells us.

"Hey, what's *that* thing?" Aiden asks.

Aiden is pointing to a huge stone statue behind us. Its body looks as long as a football field! And I think it must be as tall as the White House—which I saw one time when my family went to Washington, DC.

I'm talking *massive*.

I think the statue's body is supposed to be a lion. But its head is human, with the nose broken off.

I wonder how that happened.

"That's the Sphinx," Sofia says. She types something else into her tablet. "Which means we're in Giza, Egypt. The Sphinx is made of limestone. It . . ."

Sofia is still reading, but all I can think about is the fact that we're in *Egypt*. That's really far from school.

I want to ask Ms. Frogbottom why she's taken us to Egypt, but my teacher is busy talking to a man standing beside a group of camels that are resting in the sand.

I know better than to interrupt Ms. Frogbottom when she's talking to another grown-up. Besides, those camels look kind of gross. One of them keeps spitting out some really nasty gunk.

So I ask Oliver instead. "Why do you think Ms. Frogbottom brought us here?"

"Who knows?" Oliver answers with a shrug. "Maybe she wanted us to find out what it feels like to be in a desert. She's always saying she wants us to experience the world outside Left Turn Alleyway Elementary. And this is *waaaaayyyy* outside."

"What's to experience? It's just a whole

lot of sand." I wave a giant mosquito away from my face. "And bugs."

"We just got here. We haven't really looked around yet." Oliver smiles. "Think of it this way: as long as we stay in Egypt, we don't have to take that pop quiz."

"Sooner or later we're gonna have to take it," I say. "I'm pretty sure we're going to go back to school at some point, right?"

"We always do," Oliver assures me.

Oliver turns to Sofia, who's still reading from her tablet. "The statue was built about four thousand five hundred years ago. It's supposed to guard the tombs nearby."

"T-t-tombs?" Now she's got my attention.

"Those three huge pyramids over

there," Sofia tells me, pointing behind the Sphinx's giant body. "The mummies of some pharaohs were buried in there."

"Fair whats?" Emma asks.

"Pharaohs," Sofia corrects her. "Ancient Egyptian kings. The pyramids were built to be their tombs."

The pyramids look like they have sprung right up from the sand. The bricks are so huge, I can't imagine how ancient people without construction trucks could ever have lifted and stacked them. Especially in this heat.

If I thought they were just massive funny-shaped buildings, I'd probably want to stick around and learn about the pyramids. But now that I know they were made to hold dead kings who were turned into mummies . . . not so much.

At least I understand why Ms. Frogbottom brought us to Egypt, of all places. When I asked about a Band-Aid, I meant a little one, for my finger. But I think that started my teacher thinking about a whole different kind of bandages. *The kind of bandages mummies are wrapped in.*

I really gotta watch what I say around my teacher.

"Check out Ms. Frogbottom!" Emma shouts suddenly.

I turn around. The camels are walking toward us in a line. Our teacher is riding on the first one.

"Excuse me, Ms. Frogbottom?" I say.

"Yes?" Ms. Frogbottom looks down at me.

"I'm sorry I called out without raising my hand. I'm sorry I asked for a Band-Aid."

"That's okay, Tony," she answers.

"So we can go home now," I continue hopefully.

"Nonsense. We just got here. There's so much to see."

I had a feeling she was going to say that.

FROGBOTTOM FaCTS

★ Camels with one hump are called dromedary camels. Camels with two humps are called Bactrian camels.

★ Camels have a third eyelid that keeps the sand out—it moves back and forth like a windshield wiper.

★ Camels can run up to forty miles per hour. That's almost as fast as a car on the highway.

"Anybody know a camel's favorite nursery rhyme?" Oliver asks.

"'*Hump*ty Dumpty'!" Olivia answers. She and Oliver start to laugh. But the rest of us just groan.

"Your riddles are so bad," Emma tells the twins.

"Speaking of riddles," Ms. Frogbottom says, "I remember a movie I once saw with a group of explorers who had to solve a riddle or risk being devoured by an Egyptian Sphinx."

Gulp. "Devour" was one of our Words of the Day. It means "to eat hungrily."

"What was the riddle?" Olivia asks her.

"We're great at riddles," Oliver brags.

"This is a tough one," Ms. Frogbottom warns them.

"Bring it on," Olivia says.

"Are you nuts?" I ask Olivia. "Do you want to be devoured?"

"Relax," Oliver tells me. "Ms. Frogbottom only saw it in a movie. That thing couldn't *really* devour anything. It's made of stone. It can't even move its mouth."

Ms. Frogbottom smiles. I don't know why. Maybe she likes thinking about kids being devoured.

"Okay, here it is," Ms. Frogbottom says. "If you have me, you may desire to share me. But if you share me, you shall no longer have me."

Oh boy. What kind of a riddle is that?

A hard one. That's what kind. So hard that no one could ever answer it.

I can tell Oliver and Olivia are totally stumped. Which means . . .

We're about to be devoured.

My stomach starts to feel queasy—like there are a million butterflies flying around in there. I wrap my arms around my belly and squeeze hard, but those butterfly wings won't stop flapping.

"I know!" Sofia shouts excitedly. "It's a secret! Because if you have a secret but you share it with someone else, then it's not a secret anymore."

"Very good, Sofia!" Ms. Frogbottom compliments her.

"Hooray!" I punch my fist triumphantly into the air. "We're not getting devoured!"

"Speaking of *devouring*," Aiden says, "I'm hungry."

Aiden is the smallest kid in our class—with the biggest stomach.

"I know a great place for lunch," Ms. Frogbottom tells him. "It's just a short ride away. And our transportation is already here."

"We're going on those?" I ask, nervously pointing to the line of camels.

"Of course," Ms. Frogbottom says. "How else?"

One of the camels lowers himself to the ground. The man who brought him over helps me climb onto the camel's back.

I try not to think about how badly this camel stinks. Or how scratchy his fur is. Or about how many flies are flying around. Or—

WHOA! Suddenly the camel stands up. I hold on tight to the front of the saddle and try not to look down.

Did I mention that I'm afraid of heights?

"Sofia," Emma calls from atop her camel. "Use the camera on your tablet to take my photo."

"Emma," Ms. Frogbottom warns. "You know the rule."

"We cannot take any photos during our field trips," we all reply dutifully.

"Exactly," Ms. Frogbottom says with a smile. "If you use your senses to experience Egypt, you won't need pictures to remember this day."

My senses? Well, so far I *feel* hot. I *smell* camel stink. I *see* sand. And I *hear* bugs buzzing near my ear. That just leaves—

"Now off to lunch!" Ms. Frogbottom exclaims.

I guess I will be *tasting* things soon.

My teacher's camel begins to move across the desert sand. Somehow our camels know to follow.

Thump. Bump. Thump. Bump. My rear end is really gonna hurt after this.

"Look at that sweet black cat," Sofia says as we ride along. "He has a cute pink nose."

Black cat! *Oh no!* How can Sofia say a

black cat is sweet? Doesn't she know that black cats bring bad luck?

"You're obsessed with cats," Olivia tells her.

"I am not," Sofia argues.

Yeah, she is.

At the moment, Sofia is wearing a white

shirt decorated with little pink cats. Her earrings have cat faces on them. Back at school she's got her Hello Kitty backpack.

I think all the cat stuff started when Sofia found a lost kitten near her house. But her mother made her give it back when its owner called.

"So what if I like cats?" Sofia asks, defending herself. "In ancient Rome, soldiers traveled with cats when they went to war. Early Greek playwrights gave cats parts in their plays. Here in Egypt, people worshipped a cat goddess. That black cat could be related to one that lived with ancient Egyptian royalty. I'm lucky to have spotted him!"

SPLAT!

Just then Emma's camel lets out a big glob of spit.

It kicks its back legs.

And starts moving. *Fast.*

"Whoa!" I hear Emma shout as her camel breaks out of the line and starts galloping across the desert sand.

"Hold on, Emma!" Ms. Frogbottom calls. "I'm coming!"

Our teacher's camel starts galloping too. A moment later Ms. Frogbottom is beside Emma. She reaches over and grabs ahold of the reins on Emma's camel.

Now the two camels are galloping side by side.

Ms. Frogbottom looks like she might fall off any moment. But she isn't letting go of the reins of Emma's camel. I can see her lips moving. But I can't hear what she's saying.

And then . . .

Emma's camel comes to a stop. Just like that. So does Ms. Frogbottom's camel.

Our camels keep walking. But they stop as soon as we reach Emma and our teacher.

"Are you okay, Emma?" Ms. Frogbottom asks.

Emma looks at her hands and feet—like she's checking to see if they're still there. Then she puts her hand up to her head. "I think so," she says. "But I bet my hair's a mess."

Everybody starts laughing. Well, everybody but me. I'm in no mood to laugh.

"Black cats are *bad* luck," I say.

"They're not," Sofia insists. "That's just an old superstition."

"Are you kidding?" I ask. "Look at what just happened. You saw the cat, and then Emma's camel went crazy."

"That had nothing to do with the cat," Sofia argues. "The camel probably got bitten by a mosquito or something. Besides, no one got hurt. So that's good luck."

I look around, but I don't see the black cat anywhere. Which is just fine with me.

I don't care if Sofia is the class brain.

I don't care if she's usually right about everything.

She's wrong about black cats. I just know it.

3

"IT SMELLS WEIRD HERE," OLIVER SAYS
as Ms. Frogbottom helps him climb down
from his camel.

"We don't use the word 'weird' during
field trips, Oliver," Ms. Frogbottom
reminds him. "These smells are just different from what you're used to. That
strong scent is cumin and coriander—
some of the spices Egyptians use in their
cooking."

"I can't wait to taste the food—not just smell it!" Aiden says.

"That's the spirit, Aiden," Ms. Frogbottom says. "You can learn a lot about other people and the way they live by trying their food! It's a way of getting up close and personal."

We don't need food to do that. There are people *up close* wherever I look. This place is so crowded. Everyone seems to be in a hurry to get to the small shops and stalls on either side of this narrow stone path. The shops sell everything from T-shirts, to spices, to copper plates, to giant, colorful carpets.

"Welcome to the souk!" Ms. Frogbottom exclaims. "Follow me."

As we walk along the stone pathway,

shopkeepers call out to us, trying to get us to look at what they're selling.

"Ooh! Look!" Emma stops near a stand that sells jewelry made of clear orange stones with black things inside them. "This necklace would really bring out my eyes."

Ms. Frogbottom shakes her head. "You know the rule," she said.

"No souvenirs," Emma replies with a frown. "But those are still pretty stones."

"They're called amber," Ms. Frogbottom tells her.

"It looks like there's a *bug* in one of them," Olivia points out.

Sofia searches something on her tablet. "It says here that amber often includes parts of ancient insects, such as dung beetles. It's like they've become mummified inside the gemstone."

"Dung?" Oliver repeats. "Isn't that animal poop?"

"Yes," Ms. Frogbottom agrees. "Dung beetle babies feed on it."

Olivia giggles. "Emma, do you think poop bugs bring out your eyes?"

Emma scowls and drops that necklace, fast.

"I thought we were going to eat," Aiden interrupts.

Wow. Nothing—not even talking about bug mummies and poop—can keep Aiden from thinking about eating.

"Don't worry, Aiden," Ms. Frogbottom

assures him. "We're almost at my favorite food stall."

Aaaachoooo! I let out a big sneeze. Long strings of boogers explode from my nose.

"Hold on, Tony," Ms. Frogbottom says. "I've got tissues in my backpack."

Of course she does. What *doesn't* Ms. Frogbottom have in her backpack?

"Oh wow!" Sofia exclaims suddenly. "There's that cute black cat again."

I search around for the cat. I want to make sure I stay out of its way, so it won't cross my path and bring me bad luck.

But I don't see it. None of us do.

"*Where's* the cat?" Oliver asks Sofia.

"It was here a minute ago. Right there, at the very next stall," Sofia replies. "It

must have gone around the corner."

"I doubt it was the same cat," Olivia says. "It's a long walk from the Sphinx to the souk."

"It looked like the same cat," Sofia murmurs. "He had a pink nose."

"I think the heat has gotten to you," Aiden tells her. "You're imagining things."

"I'm *not* imagining," Sofia insists.

"Ow!"

FROGBOTTOM FACTS

★ Ancient Egyptians believed that cats were magical and would bring good luck to the people who kept them.

★ Some families dressed their cats in jewels.

★ Cats were considered so important that when they died, they were often mummified, just like the pharaohs.

Just then a man carrying a big carpet on his shoulder bangs right into Oliver.

Bam. Oliver bumps into me.

Whoops. I lose my footing. And . . .

Slam.

I fall right into one of the stalls.

Cling . . . clang . . . clunk.

Piles of pots and pans fall off the table in front of the stall.

The man selling the pots and pans

★ 46 ★

comes running out. He's yelling at me in a language I don't understand. But I can tell he's mad.

"I'm sorry," I apologize. "It wasn't my fault."

The man looks at me and grumbles.

"See?" I ask Sofia. "You just have to mention that black cat, and bad stuff happens."

Sofia rolls her eyes. "It's not the cat's fault that you're a klutz," she tells me.

Ms. Frogbottom reaches over and helps me to my feet. "I think we make a right turn," she tells us, changing the subject. "The lunch stall should be right there."

We all follow Ms. Frogbottom—well, all of us except Sofia. She has stopped to stare at a poster on the wall of a shop that sells souvenir-type stuff.

"We'd better wait for Sofia," Oliver tells Ms. Frogbottom.

Ms. Frogbottom looks over and smiles. "Oh, she's studying the hieroglyphics."

"Hi-ro whats?" Aiden asks.

"Hieroglyphics," Ms. Frogbottom repeats. "The picture alphabet that the ancient Egyptians used."

"I'm trying to memorize as many letters as I can," Sofia explains to Ms. Frogbottom. "That way, when we get home, I can use hieroglyphics as a secret code."

"You don't need to memorize every letter," Aiden tells her. "You can look hieroglyphics up on your tablet anytime you

★ 48 ★

want."

"What if I don't have my tablet with me?" Sofia points out. "Just give me a few more minutes. You know how fast I can memorize."

I know that sounds like Sofia is bragging. But she's really not. She has an *amazing* memory. She can remember *anything* she reads or sees.

Sofia once told me the name for her special kind of memory, but I can't remember what it is.

"There are a lot of letters on that

FROGBOTTOM FACT

★ A person with an eidetic memory, also known as a photographic memory, can remember things after seeing or reading them just once.

★ 49 ★

poster," Aiden whispers to Oliver and me. "We're never gonna eat."

Aiden's not whispering as quietly as he thinks, though, because Ms. Frogbottom has heard him. "We'll eat," she assures him. "Right now, in fact."

Our teacher points to a food stall a few feet away. A man is cooking meat and vegetables on a grill. The smoke from the grill has filled the air.

"All right!" Aiden cheers. "I love a good barbecue."

"Who would like grilled chicken in a pita?" Ms. Frogbottom asks.

"That sounds good," I tell her. "I'll have one."

"Me too," Oliver agrees.

"Me three," Olivia adds.

"Does anybody want to try the *ta'ameya*?" Ms. Frogbottom asks.

She points to some balls made of . . . well . . . *something*.

"It's fried white beans and spices," my teacher explains.

"I'll try," Sofia agrees. "It looks interesting."

"I'm not sure what to eat," Emma says. "It's so hard for me to make a decision."

"No kidding," Oliver jokes. I know what he means. Every day Emma has a new name, a new thing she wants to be when she grows up, and a new way to wear her hair. She can't decide on *anything*.

"Can I have one of those?" Aiden asks,

★ 51 ★

pointing to a meat sandwich.

"The *hawawshi*?" Ms. Frogbottom says. "I don't know, Aiden. It's awfully spicy. There are chili peppers in it."

"That's okay," Aiden assures her. "I've got a strong stomach."

"All right," Ms. Frogbottom agrees. "But don't say I didn't warn you." She points to the meat sandwich and gives the man some Egyptian money.

Why Ms. Frogbottom carries Egyptian money around in her backpack, I can't tell you.

"Satisfaction guaranteed or your *mummy* back," Olivia jokes.

Sometimes I don't get Olivia. Mummies are not something you should kid around about. They're too scary.

Luckily, the closest thing to a mummy we've run into on this trip is a mummified dung beetle. Which is creepy, but not super scary.

"Here you go," Ms. Frogbottom says, handing the sandwich to Aiden.

"All right!" Aiden opens his mouth and takes a huge bite of his sandwich. He chews for a minute, and then . . . "AAAAAHHHH!" He opens his mouth wide and lets his meat-covered tongue hang out of the side of his mouth. "Hot. Hot. *Soooooo* hot!"

Tears are pouring from Aiden's eyes. If he were a cartoon character, steam would be bursting out of his ears.

"I'll just have the chicken," Emma tells Ms. Frogbottom.

"I hope you all liked your lunch," Ms. Frogbottom says a few minutes later. "Isn't the souk wonderful?"

Then she reaches into her bag and pulls out the Magic Map.

Woo-hoo! We're going home. Away from all the talk about statues that can devour kids, jewelry made of dead bugs, and pyramids with mummies inside.

"We're going here," Ms. Frogbottom says.

Wait. *What?*

Ms. Frogbottom isn't pointing anywhere *near* our school. She's pointing to a long river here in Egypt. That's *not* good news for me.

Have I mentioned I'm a lousy swimmer?

Suddenly there's a giant flash of light. My body feels weightless, and I think my feet have just left the ground.

It's like I'm flying in space. And then . . .

4

"I LOVE SAILING DOWN THE NILE!" MS.
Frogbottom exclaims a while later as we're
sailing along the river in a big sailboat.
"This river makes me happy."

"She must be *really* happy," Aiden
whispers to Oliver and me. "We've been
sailing a long time."

Aiden whispers way too loudly. Once
again Ms. Frogbottom has heard him.

"Well, the Nile *is* the longest river in

the world," Ms. Frogbottom agrees. "But we're almost there."

"Where's *there*?" Olivia asks.

"You'll see," Ms. Frogbottom replies mysteriously.

Emma reaches her hand over the side of the sailboat and tries to touch the water.

"Don't do that!" I shout so loudly that I surprise even myself. "There could be crocodiles."

"Oh, come on." Emma rolls her eyes at me.

"Tony's right," Ms. Frogbottom tells her. "There are Nile crocodiles. Not many, but you never know when you might come across one."

I usually feel great when I'm right about something. But knowing that there could be a crocodile swimming nearby doesn't make me feel very good.

Sometimes I'd rather be wrong.

I look out across the river. For the longest time I've seen nothing but patches of thick, brownish-green reeds growing on either side. But now, as we get closer to the shore, I see sand again.

"Aah, wonderful!" Ms. Frogbottom

cheers. "You see those limestone hills out there? That's where many of the pharaoh mummies were buried."

"Are the mummies wrapped in bandages like in the movies?" Emma asks excitedly.

Ms. Frogbottom nods. "The ancient Egyptians wrapped dead people in specially treated bandages to make sure the bodies didn't rot. That's why mummies that are thousands of years old still have skin on their bones and hair on their heads. I can't wait for you to see their tombs."

Yuck.

"Sofia, stop looking at your tablet," Emma interrupts. "You're missing everything."

"I was reading about the lives of ancient Egyptians. I found some interesting info about mummies," Sofia answers. "Did you know that before the ancient Egyptians wrapped a dead member of the royal family in bandages, they took out his stomach, intestines, lungs, and liver? They stored them in jars."

Aiden grabs his stomach. "Maybe I shouldn't have eaten all that food at the souk."

Aiden isn't the only one who feels sick. All this talk about jars filled with livers and intestines is making me pretty queasy too.

"You can read about that later," Emma tells Sofia. "We're here *now*. Lala Radala says it's important to experience real life."

Lala Radala is Emma's favorite singer. Emma is always telling us about things Lala has said. Usually no one cares. But today Sofia actually listens. "I'm running low on battery anyway," she says as she shuts down her tablet and looks toward the shore.

"Oh my goodness!" Sofia exclaims. "There he is again!"

"There *who* is?" Aiden wonders.

"The black cat with the pink nose," Sofia replies. "He's right there, walking on the shore. I think he's following us."

"I don't see anything," Emma says.

"Me neither," Olivia agrees.

"He was just there a second ago," Sofia insists.

This whole cat thing is really getting strange. On the one hand, Sofia doesn't usually make stuff up.

On the other hand, it's odd that none of the rest of us have spotted so much as a cat's *tail*.

But if Sofia isn't lying, then there's a black cat wandering around that only she can see.

A cat that can magically travel all over Egypt on *its* own.

Which is impossible. *Isn't it?*

Splash!

Before I can sort it all out, a big wave splashes over the side of the boat.

The wave seemed to come out of nowhere. And now there are more of them. The boat is rocking back and forth wildly.

So is my stomach.

Crash!

"Hold on!" Ms. Frogbottom calls out as another wave crashes onto the boat.

Splat! A fish flies up and hits me right in the face.

Yuck! That fish is slimy. And stinky.

The boat's captain jumps into action. He pulls at the ropes that turn the sails on our boat and steers us out of the way of another giant wave. A moment later we're back sailing on smooth water.

"You okay, Tony?" Oliver asks me. "You look green."

I'm *not* okay. I'm still queasy. And I'm worried.

"Stupid black cat." I bite my lower lip nervously.

"Really?" Sofia asks me. "You're going to blame waves on that poor sweet cat?"

"There is *no* cat." Oliver frowns at Sofia. "Stop goofing around. You're freaking Tony out. Look at him. He's gonna bite a hole in his face."

Thump. Thump. Thud. Just then the boat comes to a stop at the dock. "Welcome to Luxor, home to the Valley of the Kings," Ms. Frogbottom says excitedly. "The gateway to the afterlife."

Afterlife? I've never heard that word before.

But I can pretty much figure out what
it means.

5

"ARE YOU GETTING ANY SIGNAL ON YOUR tablet?" Olivia asks Sofia, who is staring at her tablet once again. "Or are we in a *dead* zone?"

I don't think Luxor is any place to joke about. There are *a lot* of tombs here. They're built right into the white stone hills. Unlike the ones near the Sphinx, you'd hardly notice them at all—if they didn't have lines of tourists waiting to go inside.

"You'd think pharaohs would be buried in fancier places," Emma says. "It looks like the people who buried the kings here wanted to *hide* their tombs."

"Maybe that's because they didn't want people to find the tombs and steal what's been buried *with* the pharaohs," Sofia says. "I *am* getting a signal. And according to this website I found, the mummies are buried with jewels, pottery, games, furniture, weapons, and food."

"Why would a dead person need that stuff?" Aiden asks.

"Ancient Egyptians believed they would use them in the next life," Sofia says. "The *afterlife*. It also says—"

Sofia stops reading and stares at me.

"It also says what?" I ask her.

"Never mind," Sofia says.

"No, really, what does it say?" I insist.

"I don't think you want to hear this, Tony," she tells me. From the tone of her voice, I believe her.

"Well, he might not want to, but *I* do," Aiden says.

"Tell us," Oliver pleads. "Tony can cover his ears."

Which I do. Unfortunately, I still hear

what Sofia says next: "If anyone disturbs the tomb of a pharaoh, they will meet bad luck, illness, or even death. They'll be cursed."

Boy, I wish she hadn't said that.

I wish I hadn't *heard* that.

Now all I can think about are curses.

And mummies.

And bad-luck black cats that bring problems wherever they go.

"Come on, Tony," Oliver says. "You don't believe what Sofia just read, do you?"

"It only happens in the movies," Olivia adds.

"People who make movies have to get their ideas from somewhere," I tell them. "Maybe from someone who was really

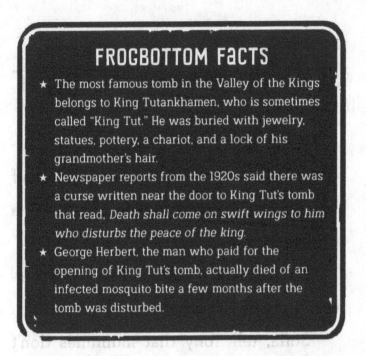

FROGBOTTOM FACTS

★ The most famous tomb in the Valley of the Kings belongs to King Tutankhamen, who is sometimes called "King Tut." He was buried with jewelry, statues, pottery, a chariot, and a lock of his grandmother's hair.

★ Newspaper reports from the 1920s said there was a curse written near the door to King Tut's tomb that read, *Death shall come on swift wings to him who disturbs the peace of the king.*

★ George Herbert, the man who paid for the opening of King Tut's tomb, actually died of an infected mosquito bite a few months after the tomb was disturbed.

captured by a mummy that came back to life?"

"Tony's right," Emma agrees.

"I am?" I wasn't expecting *that*.

"Sure," Emma says. "Lots of movies are based on things that really happen. I should know. I'm writing my own screenplay. It's for a disaster movie."

"What do you know about disasters?" Olivia asks her.

"What about the time I told my hairdresser I wanted a trim but she cut off four inches?" Emma replies. "That was a disaster."

"Mummies are scarier than hairdressers," I say nervously.

"Sofia, tell Tony that mummies don't really come back to life," Oliver urges.

We all turn around to hear what the class brain has to say about this.

There's just one problem.

Sofia isn't here. She has disappeared.

"SOFIA! WHERE ARE YOU?" I CALL NERVOUSLY.

"This isn't funny."

And it's not. Not one bit.

It's also not like Sofia to play this sort of trick on anyone. That's something Olivia would do.

Except Olivia is standing right here. And Sofia is gone.

"Excuse me, Ms. Frogbottom? Did you see which way Sofia went?" Aiden asks.

Our teacher is busy having a conversation with a camel. She's talking, and the camel is nodding its head, like it understands every word she says.

"Oh dear, has Sofia wandered off again?" Ms. Frogbottom asks with a heavy sigh. "She and I will have to have a chat when we get back to school."

I wouldn't want to be Sofia when that happens. Ms. Frogbottom's chats aren't as friendly as they might sound.

Our teacher reaches into her backpack and pulls out a giant prickly cactus leaf for the camel to chomp on. "She can't have gone far. I'll look by that tomb over there on the right. You kids look near the tombs to the left. Just stay

where I can keep an eye on you."

As we walk off, Aiden starts talking excitedly. "We should pretend to be detectives, like in the mystery book I took out of the library last week." He sounds like he thinks this is the coolest game in the world.

But it's *not* a game. Or a book. It's real life.

"How do we pretend to be detectives?" Oliver sounds like he thinks this is a cool game too.

I don't understand my friends.

"We look for clues," Aiden replies. "Like Sofia's footprints in the sand."

I look down. There are a lot of footprints. Many people visit the Valley of the Kings.

"Sofia's feet would be smaller than these," Aiden says, pointing to one set of footprints. "And—"

Before Aiden can finish what he's saying, the wind starts blowing. It's the kind of wind you can actually hear. Sand is flying everywhere. There's no way we can search for Sofia in this.

It's almost as if someone is warning us *not* to look for her.

But who would do that?

No one. Unless—

"What if this sand *is* Sofia?" I shout over the wind. "What if she disturbed a tomb, and the curse turned her to sand? What if she's warning us not to look any further? What if—"

I don't get to finish my thought, because a blast of sand blows into my mouth. It's like someone is trying to shut me up.

Oh no! What if I swallowed some *Sofia* sand?

A few seconds later the wind stops. Just as suddenly as it started. "Do you think I could be right?" I ask my friends.

★ 77 ★

"A curse that turns people into sand?" Olivia replies. "Not a chance. That's impossible."

I guess it is. *And yet* . . .

"There are five of us," Aiden interrupts. "Let's split up. We'll cover more ground that way."

Split up? No way. "I'm not going anywhere near those tombs by myself. There are mummies in there," I say.

FROGBOTTOM FaCTS

★ There are more than sixty tombs in the Valley of the Kings. While a few are open to the public, most are not.

★ Some of the tombs actually have graffiti on them— *written by ancient Roman and Greek visitors.* Even back then, the Valley of the Kings was a big tourist attraction.

"Tony's right," Oliver agrees. "We'd better stick together."

"Fine. We'll go together." Aiden doesn't sound happy. "But it's gonna take us longer to find Sofia that way."

If we find her.

I look around at all the people who are waiting to get into the pharaohs' tombs. Personally, I would never wait in a line to go see a mummy. But it's just the kind of thing Sofia would do—so she could learn something new about ancient Egyptians.

Only, Sofia isn't waiting in any of the lines.

"Do you think she's already inside one of the tombs?" Oliver wonders.

"I doubt it," Aiden replies. "She's only been missing a few minutes. Look at how long those lines are."

"She probably saw some cat and went off to play with it," Emma suggests.

"If that's true, she could be anywhere," Aiden points out. "Maybe we should try looking over there, away from all these people."

I follow my friends up a sand dune. It's hard to walk. My shoes are filling with sand, which makes them really heavy. But I keep trudging. I won't be left behind.

We're looking everywhere. Sofia is nowhere to be found. We could be here a long time. We may even be stuck in Egypt way past school dismissal.

My mom will freak out if I'm not back by dismissal.

As for me, I'm *already* freaking out. But not because we're going to be late. I'm freaking out because I just realized that Sofia isn't the only one who has disappeared into the gateway to the afterlife.

Someone else is missing too!

7

"WHERE'S AIDEN?" I SHOUT.

"He's right—" Oliver begins. Then he stops and looks around. "He was here a minute ago."

"The mummy got him!" I exclaim. "I knew it."

"Don't be ridiculous," Oliver tells me.

Tap. Tap. Tap. I feel someone touching my shoulder.

"AAAHHHH!" I let out a scream so

loud that the pharaohs can probably hear me in the afterlife.

Then I hear giggling. I'd know that laugh anywhere. "Olivia," I groan. "Why would you do that?"

"Can't you take a joke, Tony?" she asks between giggles.

"Not now I can't."

"Relax," Olivia replies. "Aiden probably went off to search for Sofia on his own like he wanted to do in the first place."

"Do you think he's up there?" Emma points to some far-off hills.

"He's been gone, like, two seconds," Olivia replies. "He couldn't have gotten up there that fast unless he had wings."

"Maybe there's an Egyptian monster that has wings," I say. "And maybe, when we weren't looking, the monster swooped down and grabbed Aiden, and now the monster is flying him back to its nest somewhere far away, and now—" I clap my own hand over my mouth. I gotta stop talking. I'm scaring myself.

"Where do you come up with this

stuff?" Oliver asks me. "Aiden's probably just searching around some of these tombs."

That makes sense. I know it does. But not everything that happens to the kids in Ms. Frogbottom's class always makes sense. Starting with the fact that there's a perfectly normal-looking map that magically flies us all over the world.

"Now we gotta look for him, too," Emma says angrily. She starts heading toward a group of tombs. "Come on."

We trudge over to where there are people lined up to go inside the tombs. We walk around, searching each and every person in line. But there's no Aiden. Or Sofia. In fact, there's not a kid in sight.

"We're never going to find them in this crowd," Olivia groans.

"Don't say that," I plead. "We *have* to find them."

"Hey, you guys!" Suddenly I hear a kid calling out. "Over here."

"That's Aiden," Olivia says.

"How do you know?" I ask her.

"Because it sounds like Aiden," Olivia tells me.

"It could be a mummy *pretending* to sound like Aiden," I answer.

"Right, like there's such a thing as a mummy that does kid imitations." Olivia laughs.

"Imitations are very hard to do," Emma tells her. "We practice them in my acting classes. Do you think mummies take acting classes?"

"No, I don't," Olivia replies. "That's Aiden. Come on."

"Come on! Hurry up!" the voice says.

We follow the sound of the voice around the bend. Sure enough, there's Aiden. He's standing beside a small doorway.

"Look what I found," he says.

"A tomb," Oliver said. "Big deal. There are a bunch of them around here."

"None this small," Aiden says. "Or this tucked away. There are no tourists or lines."

"Also no Sofia," I point out.

"True," Aiden admits. "But the door is open. Which could mean someone went inside. It's a small door—no average-size grown-up could fit through here."

"It had to be a kid," Oliver says.

"Exactly," Aiden agrees.

"Or it could be a kid mummy who opened the door and went *outside*," I suggest.

"I'm pretty sure Sofia is in there," Aiden insists. "We should go find her."

"I'm not going," I answer nervously. "You heard what happens to people who disturb a tomb."

"We're not going to disturb anything," Aiden assures me. "We're just going to go in there, get Sofia, and leave."

"Ms. Frogbottom said to stay where she can see us," I remind him. "She can't see us inside a tomb."

Nobody says anything. They know I'm right.

"We're not even sure she's in there," I continue. "So why go?"

"Because we don't have a choice," Oliver tells me. "It would be a disaster if we had to go back to school without Sofia."

"It would be an even bigger disaster if Ms. Frogbottom refuses to go back without Sofia," Aiden adds.

They've got me there.

"Okay," I agree. "But let's make it quick."

"I'll go in first," Aiden tells us. "You guys follow close behind."

Aiden pushes the door open a little wider and heads into the tomb. We follow in a tight, straight line. The light from outside is streaming through the open door. It shines onto some paintings on the walls.

"Whoa!" Emma points to brightly colored orange-and-yellow drawings of ancient Egyptian women. "That paint looks like it's mixed with real gold."

I'm not looking at the paintings of the women. I'm looking at carvings of small birds, feet, and feathery-looking things that were on the hieroglyphics poster Sofia was studying at the souk.

The hieroglyphics are carved above a brightly colored drawing of a man with a bird's head. The bird-man is wrapping a mummy in bandages.

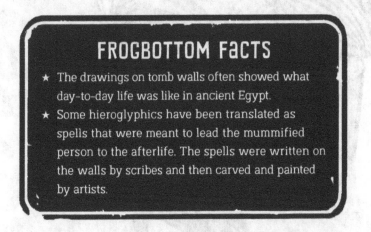

My body starts to shake. I'm pretty sure that means we're not the only ones inside this tomb. And I don't mean Sofia.

I mean a mummy. Because even though we haven't seen him yet, there's a really good chance some rich person was buried in here.

Aaachooooo! Suddenly I let out a massive sneeze. Boogers fly all over the place.

Slam!

The door to the tomb blows shut. Almost like by magic.

Or by *curse.*

Either way, it's bad. Because now *it's completely dark!*

"Tony! You sneezed the door shut!" Emma yells at me.

"I didn't sneeze *that* hard."

"Maybe it got windy again outside," Oliver says, defending me.

"I don't think it was the wind," I say nervously. "I bet someone, or some*thing*, closed it for us."

"It's not a big deal," Aiden says. "We just have to push the door open."

"Okay. *Oomf.*" I hear Oliver grunting in the darkness as he pushes at the stone door. "This door is heavy," he adds. "Can you guys help me?"

We all walk toward the sound of Oliver's voice.

"Okay. On the count of three let's

push," Aiden says. "One . . . two . . . THREE!"

Oomf.

Erg.

Argh.

We're all pushing, hard.

But the door doesn't open.

"I think it opens the other way," Oliver tells Aiden.

"So pull it," Aiden replies.

"I can't," Oliver says. "There's no door-knob."

What?

"Did you just say what I think you said?" I ask Oliver.

"N-n-no doorknob?" Emma repeats nervously.

"That's what I said," Oliver replies.

We all start pounding on the door.

"HELP!" I cry.

"Somebody get us out of here!" Emma shrieks.

"Is there anybody there?" Olivia calls.

Nobody answers.

Which can only mean one terrible . . . horrible . . . really rotten thing.

WE'RE TRAPPED!

"WE'RE GOING TO BE STUCK IN HERE FOREVER."

I am starting to cry.

"We can get out of this," Aiden insists. "Give me a minute to come up with an idea."

"I don't want to hear any more of your ideas," Emma tells Aiden. "Your not-so-brilliant idea is what got us into this mess."

"What are you talking about?" Aiden asks her.

"You told us to follow you into the tomb," Olivia explains. "*That's* what she's talking about."

Sniff. Sniff.

Oh great. Now my nose is running.

I wish I brought tissues. It's kind of gross wiping your nose with your sleeve. But what choice do I have?

Scratch. Scratch. Now my arms are itchy.

A leaky nose and an itchy arm. I'm sure I've felt like this before. But I can't remember when.

"It's really *Sofia's* fault," Aiden argues. "She's the one who ran off on her own and broke the rules."

"Ms. Frogbottom sounded really mad

about that," Emma says. "She might even send a note home to Sofia's parents."

"She might send a note home to all our parents," I add as I sniff and scratch. "We didn't listen either. We didn't stay where she could see us."

"If I get in trouble for this, I'm gonna be so mad at Sofia," Aiden grumbles.

Sniff. Scratch . . .

Wait! I know the last time I felt like this. I got an allergic reaction from playing with my aunt Lucy's cat, Whiskers.

Did I mention that I'm allergic to cats? Probably not. Because I forgot all about it, until just this minute.

I remember sneezing at the souk, when Sofia said she saw a black cat at the very next stall. That cat would have been close enough to make me start feeling allergic.

"There's a cat in here somewhere," I tell the others.

"I told you guys that Sofia followed a cat," Emma boasts.

"What cat?" Olivia demands. "I never saw any cat."

"Me either," Oliver adds.

"I'm telling you there's a cat," I argue. *Aaachooo.*

"No way, Tony!" Olivia insists. "Your nose is always leaking."

"Is not!"

"Stop fighting!" Aiden yells out into the darkness. "We have to work together as a team to solve this case. It's the only way

we're going to find Sofia and get out of here."

"So what should we do, *together*?" I ask Aiden.

"For starters, we can't risk losing anybody else," Aiden says. "We should all join hands with the people on either side of us to make sure we don't get separated. And whatever you do, **DON'T LET GO**."

I reach in front of me and grab one of my classmate's hands. It's warm, wet, and clammy, just like mine. My hands always get clammy when I'm scared.

I wish I knew whose hand I was holding. But I can't see a thing.

I reach behind and grab the hand of the classmate standing behind me. This hand is actually kind of dry and scratchy. I have to tell whoever this is about the creamy lotion my mother puts on me when I get dry skin in the winter.

And I will. As soon as I can see whose hand I'm holding.

"Now move slowly," Aiden tells us. "We don't want to trip over anything in the dark."

As we start to walk in a line through the tomb of doom, I can feel my nose running. My arms are itchy too. But I don't dare wipe my nose or scratch my arms. That would mean letting go of someone's hand. And I'm not doing that.

"Hey! What's that?" I hear Oliver's voice.

I know exactly what he's talking about. A mysterious light has suddenly appeared out of nowhere.

My heart starts pounding so hard, it feels like it's going to bust out of my chest. I've never heard of a mummy that glowed in the dark.

Which means there could be a totally different kind of scary monster inside this tomb!

"That's the light from Sofia's tablet," Aiden suggests.

My heart pounds a little less.

"Sofia!" Olivia calls. "Come out here!"

The blue light moves up and down.

But there's no Sofia.

"I don't think that's Sofia," I say. "I think

it's a monster! Maybe even a more dangerous monster than a mummy! And it's gonna get us because we're trapped in here!"

"It's Sofia," Aiden insists.

The blue light glows a little brighter. It gets a little larger.

The glow-in-the-dark monster is getting closer.

And closer.

And—

"SOFIA!" I shout with relief. I can tell it's really her because she's using her tablet as a flashlight. Just like Aiden said.

"Am I glad to see you guys," she says. "I need your help finding the black cat. I saw him run in here."

We're trapped in the tomb of doom, and all Sofia can think about is a cat?

Now that Sofia is shining a light on things, I can see my friends again.

Aiden looks proud that he figured out where Sofia was.

Emma is looking at the paintings on the wall.

Oliver and Olivia are giving each other reassuring smiles. It's a twin thing, I guess.

Hey! Wait a minute. . . .

If Sofia is holding her tablet, and Aiden, Emma, Oliver, and Olivia are all standing in front of me . . .

Then who is standing behind me?

Whose cool, scratchy, dry hand have I been holding?

AAAAAAAHHHHHHHHH!

9

"IT'S THE MUMMY!" MY VOICE ECHOES through the tomb. *Mummy... mummy... mummy...*

Sofia shines her flashlight in my direction.

Everybody turns to stare. Then they start screaming too. Because standing right there... next to me... is a REAL MUMMY!

And I'm holding his hand! His cold, dry, scratchy, *bandaged* hand.

I drop that mummy's hand and start to run.

I have no idea where I'm going. I just know I want to get away from the bandaged kid as fast as I can. At least I *think* the mummy is a kid. He sure doesn't look like a grown-up. He's kind of short.

I'm not the only one running. My classmates are right there with me, trying to find some way out of this tomb. Luckily, Sofia is shining her tablet's flashlight. We can see where we're going now.

*Un*luckily, what we see is creepy—like the four jars on a shelf near the mummy's empty coffin. His intestines, liver, stomach, and lungs are in there.

That makes me want to puke. Only, I can't stop to puke now. The mummy is right behind us.

For a dead kid wrapped in bandages, that mummy sure runs fast.

We hide behind a giant pile of clay pots. But the mummy finds us.

So we start running again. This time down a long hallway lined with pictures on the wall and stone sculptures of pharaohs.

"Everybody, freeze!" Aiden shouts.

Huh? This is no time to play human statues.

Although, maybe if we all stay very, very still, the mummy will think we're actual statues and run right past us.

Aiden's idea is not a bad one. Especially since it's our *only* idea.

I pose just like one of the men in the drawings on the wall, and freeze.

Sofia turns off her flashlight. Not that it matters. I bet the mummy can see in the dark. He'd have to. There are no lights in this place.

Lub-dub. Lub-dub. Lub-dub. My heart is pounding.

The mummy's footsteps are coming closer.

And somehow, *miraculously*, the mummy runs right past us.

I can't believe it. Aiden's plan worked! That mummy actually thought we were ancient Egyptian statues. I guess mummies aren't too bright.

Aaachooooooo! Uh-oh. That was some big sneeze.

Not one of my friends says "gesundheit." Probably because they're mad at me for giving us away. Statues never sneeze.

From the sound of the mummy's footsteps, he's figured that out. He's coming back this way.

So we zoom into another room in the tomb of doom. Sofia shines her tablet light all around for a better look at things.

In one corner I see plates and what I think are a few clay pots. In another corner there are some jars and a table. The walls are decorated with drawings of women with baskets of food.

"I think this is a dining room for the mummy to use in the afterlife," Sofia says.

"It's a big dining room for just one mummy," Oliver adds.

"I'm getting kind of hungry," Aiden says.

Hungry? Now? I can't believe this guy.

If we really are trapped, the mummy will have Aiden to keep him company at dinnertime in the afterlife.

"Hey! That's it!" I shout suddenly.

"What's it?" Oliver asks me.

"I think the mummy lured Sofia in here so he could have someone to hang out with. He's probably been lonely the past few thousand years."

"Nobody *lured* me in here," Sofia argues. "I was rescuing a cat."

"It could be a magical cat," I explain. "Sent by the mummy to trick you into visiting him."

My classmates stare at me. "It could happen," I insist.

Before anyone can argue, the mummy hurries into the room and grabs a small pot. He holds it out to us.

I think he's trying to offer us food.

From three thousand years ago.

No, thanks.

We rush past him and out of his ancient Egyptian dining room.

The mummy lets out a deep growl. He sounds sad. And mad.

We run faster down a long hallway, with Sofia's flashlight lighting the way.

The next thing I know, we're back in that room with the empty mummy coffin and the jars filled with the mummy's intestines and stuff.

"This is my least favorite room in the tomb of doom!" I cry out.

"I'd feel a lot better if that mummy were back in his coffin," Oliver adds.

"Maybe we can trick him into climbing back in," Aiden suggests. "He seems pretty easily fooled. He thought we were statues, right?"

"Until one of the statues sneezed." Olivia glares at me.

"I couldn't help it," I insist.

"I don't think we'll need to fool him." Sofia shines her flashlight onto the lid of the mummy's coffin. "There's an easier way to get the mummy back into his sarcophagus."

"Back into his *what*?" Oliver asks her.

"Sarcophagus," Sofia repeats. "It's what you call this kind of stone coffin. You see this picture writing on the lid? It's a riddle."

"How do you know?" Emma asks her.

"I remember some of these letters from the poster at the souk," Sofia explains.

"I would have remembered even more if Aiden hadn't wanted to eat so badly."

We all look at Aiden.

"What?" he asks. "I was hungry."

"When we were on the boat, I found a webpage that translates words from Coptic to English," Sofia continues. "That should help."

"What's Coptic?" Emma asks.

"The language some ancient Egyptians spoke."

Sometimes it's annoying when Sofia acts like she's so much smarter than the rest of us just because she memorizes things easily. But right now Sofia can act as smart as she likes—as long as she gets us out of here.

"I think this says, 'Whoever solves the

riddle of the fire returns the mummy to where he will forever retire,'" Sofia tells us.

"That sounds good," I say. "What's the riddle?"

Sofia studies the strange picture writing for a while. Finally she reads, "'I am tall when I am young but short when I am old. What am I?'"

Huh?

"I have no idea," Oliver says.

"Look it up on your tablet," Emma suggests. "I'm sure somebody figured it out before us."

"I'm barely getting any signal because we're underground," Sofia replies. "It could take a while."

"We don't have a while," Olivia adds.

"I hear the mummy coming."

"He's going to keep us here forever!" I cry out. "We'll have nothing to eat but rotten ancient food."

"Petrified," Sofia says.

"Of course I'm petrified," I tell her. "Aren't you?"

"I meant the *food* is petrified," she explains. "Turned to stone."

"Stop talking about food, and solve this riddle," I plead.

"I don't know the answer," Sofia admits. "And we've got more to be afraid of than just the mummy. I'm down to two percent battery on my tablet. We're going to be in the dark any minute now."

Gulp.

"TOO BAD WE DON'T HAVE ANY CANDLES,"
Oliver says.

"It wouldn't matter if we did," Emma
points out. "We don't have matches to
light them."

"I'm not even allowed to use matches,"
I add.

"What's the difference?" Aiden asks.
"A candle would burn down and go out.
We'd still be left in the dark."

I feel like crying. I don't want to be left in the dark forever with an angry mummy. But I will be. Because none of us will ever figure out that riddle.

"Aiden!" Sofia exclaims. "You're a genius."

"I am?" Aiden asks. "I mean *of course* I am. Wait. *Why* am I a genius?"

"You solved the riddle," Sofia answers. "A candle starts out tall but gets shorter the longer it melts."

Eeerggghhhh!

Suddenly we hear a loud squeal. Like air being sucked out of a balloon.

It's the mummy! *He's back!*

My heart is pounding. My knees are knocking. I have goose pimples everywhere. He's going to grab one of us. I just know it.

Except he doesn't.

He walks right past us. And climbs into his coffin.

SLAM! The lid shuts tight.

"We did it!" I cheer excitedly.

SLAM! Just then, another loud noise echoes through the tomb.

"What was that?" Emma asks nervously.

"I don't know." Oliver points toward the opening to the room. "But it came from out there."

Sofia walks over to take a look. "Oh my! Another mummy."

"A-a-a-nother mummy?" I stammer nervously.

"Relax, Tony," Sofia says. "It's sealed in its sarcophagus. Look."

We walk toward the glow of Sofia's tablet. She's shining it on a mini coffin that's painted to look like a black cat. *With a little pink nose.*

"I knew it!" I say. "The mummy sent its cat to lure Sofia in here."

"But how?" Emma asks. "The door won't open from inside."

"Maybe someone discovered this tomb before us," I suggest. "Maybe he disturbed the tomb and woke the mummy and his cat. Maybe he was able to escape, but left the door open. Maybe—"

"That's a lot of maybes," Olivia says, interrupting.

"It could happen," I reply.

"It doesn't really matter what happened *then*," Aiden tells us. "We need to get out *now*. The door is that way."

Sofia aims her tablet light, and we start

walking toward the door. The closer we get, the better I feel.

Until Olivia says, "But the door opens in and there's no doorknob, remember?"

Oh. Right.

I grab my stomach and squeeze hard. Those nervous butterflies are back. And they're flapping around like crazy.

"We may not need a doorknob." Sofia points her tablet flashlight to up above the doorway. "There are more hieroglyphics up there. It could be another riddle."

"What does it say?" I ask.

Sofia studies the pictures. "That's strange. It doesn't really make sense."

"Tell us anyway," Emma urges her.

"Okay," Sofia says. "'What runs but never walks, and has no feet?'"

"That can't be it," Aiden tells her. "You must have remembered the letters wrong."

"I don't remember things wrong," Sofia insists.

"Then we're in trouble," I tell her. "Because you can't run without feet."

"Try again," Aiden tells her.

Sofia rolls her eyes. "Fine. But it's not gonna change." She points the light up at the hieroglyphics. "You see those two feet? That means 'walk,' and—"

Before Sofia can read the rest of the message again, everything goes dark. Again.

Gulp. Again.

"I'm out of battery!" Sofia exclaims.

"And we're out of luck!" I sob. Tears are running down my cheeks, and . . .

Hey. Wait a minute.

"I know the answer!" I exclaim. "It's tears. Tears run, but they never walk. And they don't have feet."

I stand there, fully expecting the door to swing open and the sunlight to hit my face. I can't wait to be the hero of Class 4A.

But the door doesn't open.

"Maybe you read the riddle wrong," Aiden tells Sofia.

"Nope," Sofia disagrees. "Because Tony's right."

Okay. Now things are so bad, even the class brain is losing it. I'm clearly *not* right. If I were, we'd be out of here.

"Except maybe the answer is 'water,'" Sofia continues.

The door to the tomb of doom swings open.

"I'm out of here!" I exclaim as I make a run for it.

THUMP. A moment later the door swings shut.

Quickly I count my classmates—Sofia, Aiden, Emma, Oliver, and Olivia. We're all here. Outside. Safe.

"I'm glad you figured it out," I tell Sofia.

"You had the idea before I did," she replies. "I just came up with a different kind of liquid."

I smile proudly. It feels good to be the

hero who saved Class 4A. Or co-hero, anyway.

"I'm really ready to leave Egypt," I tell my classmates.

"Me too," Oliver agrees. "Not that it hasn't been interesting, but you know . . ."

"Oh, we *know*," Olivia assures him. "This has been like all of Ms. Frogbottom's field trips. Kind of cool and—"

"Kind of scary," I say, finishing her sentence. "*Really* scary."

"I have to get home soon," Emma agrees. "I've got dance class this afternoon. Mademoiselle Lily gets mad if you're late."

"She sounds like Ms. Frogbottom," Olivia says.

"If Ms. Frogbottom wore a tutu," Emma replies.

I don't even want to think about what *that* would look like.

"Speaking of Ms. Frogbottom," Aiden points out, "we should get back to her."

I try really hard not to fall as we race down the sand dune. It's harder walking down than it was going up.

Just as we're reaching the bottom, I spot Ms. Frogbottom. She's walking near the tombs, looking around. Probably for us.

What a relief! I'm actually *glad* to see my teacher.

"Hi, Ms. Frogbottom!" I shout as I run toward her.

"There you are," Ms. Frogbottom greets us sternly. "You had me worried. I thought I told you to stay where I could see you."

"But there was this weird mum—" I begin to explain.

Ms. Frogbottom shoots me a look.

"Not *weird*," I correct myself. "But strange."

"We got *wrapped up* in finding Sofia," Olivia adds. She laughs at her own joke.

Ms. Frogbottom isn't laughing. "We'll chat about this later," she tells us firmly. "Now we need to get back in time for dismissal."

Ms. Frogbottom reaches into her pack and pulls out the Magic Map. She points to a picture of our school.

A white light flashes all around us. My body feels weightless, and I think my feet have just left the ground.

It's like I'm flying in space. And then . . .

11

I HAVE NEVER BEEN SO GLAD TO SEE MY mom in my whole life! She's waiting in the school yard at dismissal time. Right by the basketball courts. Just like always.

"Did you do anything interesting in school today?" my mom asks as we start walking home together.

"We learned about mummies and hieroglyphics and stuff," I answer her.

"It was just a regular school day."

Which it *was*.

At least for the kids in Ms. Frogbottom's class.

WORDS YOU HEAR ON a FiELD TRiP TO EGYPT

chariot: A two-wheeled horse-drawn cart used in ancient battles

Coptic: A language spoken by ancient Egyptians

desert: A dry area of land with very little plant life

hawawshi: A traditional Egyptian dish made with minced meat that has been spiced with onions, parsley, and chili peppers

hieroglyphics: Pictures or symbols used for writing

mummy: The body of a dead human or

animal that was preserved when special priests removed some of its internal organs, covered it with natron (salt) and wrapped it in bandages

pharaoh: A ruler in ancient Egypt

pyramid: A large structure in Egypt that is usually built on a square base, and has sides that meet at a point at the top

tomb: A place created to hold a dead person

sarcophagus: A coffin, often made of stone, that is sometimes decorated with sculpture, paintings, and writing

Sphinx: A giant limestone statue with the body of a lion and the head of a pharaoh, built forty-five hundred years ago

souk: An Arab marketplace

ta'ameya: Egyptian street food made with fava beans and often served in a pita with tomatoes, onions, and tahini sauce

WHAT HAPPENS IN THE NEXT FANTASTICAL ADVENTURE?

MS. FROGBOTTOM'S
FIELD TRIPS

LONG TIME, NO SEA MONSTER

NANCY KRULIK
NEW YORK TIMES BESTSELLING AUTHOR